T0149385

MAUREEN ATCHESON

Benjamin's Quest

WESTBOW
PRESS®
A DIVISION OF THOMAS NELSON
& ZONDERVAN

WestBow Press books may be ordered through booksellers or by contacting:

WestBow Press
A Division of Thomas Nelson & Zondervan
1663 Liberty Drive
Bloomington, IN 47403
www.westbowpress.com
1 (866) 928-1240

ISBN: 978-1-5127-7640-9 (sc)
ISBN: 978-1-5127-7641-6 (e)

Library of Congress Control Number: 2017902629

Print information available on the last page.

WestBow Press rev. date: 10/1/2019

I dedicate this book to my son and daughter,
Colin and Laura, whom I deeply love.

Illustrations by Alex Nekrasovsky.

CHAPTER 1

Benjamin Frog heaved a great sigh as he sat one night on his lily pad.

"Why was he sighing?" you might ask.

Well, he was feeling very sad.

His lily pad was floating on a beautiful pond in the middle of a dense forest. During the day, bees buzzed and butterflies and dragon-flies floated and fluttered happily about. The pool was surrounded by lush vegetation. On its banks grew sweet smelling lilacs, hollyhocks, daisies, buttercups and dandelions. The pond also displayed the changing colours of the sky by day and the cascades of stars and the moon by night.

There were families of beaver, otter, ducks and swans living healthily and undisturbed around the pond.

Benjamin was friendly with all the animals who lived there and was liked and respected by all his neighbours.

"Benjamin," Mrs. Duck would say, "little Bertie Duck is sick today. Would you babysit him for me while I go shopping?"

"Of course, Mrs. Duck," Benjamin would reply, "I'd be glad to."

Often, when Mrs. Beaver was having a problem with one of her active children, she would swim out to the lily pad on which Benjamin usually liked to sit.

"Benjamin, have you any idea what I could do about little Billy Beaver? He keeps swimming out of the house and chewing poor Mrs. Duck's laundry line. Her nice clean clothes land on the ground, or sometimes on top of her ducklings!" Benjamin would always listen carefully and would give the best advice he could.

I'm sure you're wondering why, in the middle of all this beauty and with all these friends, he was unhappy. I'll tell you the answer to that. Benjamin had one problem; although he had lots of different animal friends, he often felt very lonely, because he was the only frog living on the pond. He would sit on his lily pad, sigh and say sadly to himself, "I wish I had a froggy friend." Sometimes he croaked loudly, hoping for an answering call, but it never came.

One night, as he was sitting on his lily pad looking at the stars, he was startled to see a glowing light over to one side of the pond. He turned his head to look, and saw a most beautiful lady, wearing a long white dress, walking along holding a brightly shining lantern. She stopped and stood on the bank of the pond, facing Benjamin. He had never experienced anything like this on his pond before. He had no idea where she had come from or why she was there. He was about to leap from his pad and hide under the water, when she smiled at him.

"Have no fear Benjamin," she said. "The king is well pleased with you."

"H--h--how do you know my name?" stammered Benjamin. "Wh—wh—what king? H—h—how does he know me?"

"He sees and knows all things," replied the lady. "He is called by the name the Great King. He knows that you are courageous and good and he has need of you." Upon hearing this, Benjamin stood up tall – as tall as a frog can stand - stuck out his chest and stated bravely, "If the Great King requires my services, I will certainly answer

his summons; but how can I help him if I don't know where to find him? And who are you?"

"My name is Obedience. The king knew he could rely on you to respond this way, Benjamin. He asks you to follow me and all will be revealed."

With that, the lady turned and began to walk through the flowers and grasses growing around the pond, along a path Benjamin had never seen before. He hopped off his pad, swam to the shore and followed Obedience, still feeling afraid, because he wondered where she was leading him and what he would find when he got there.

CHAPTER 2

Obedience was able to move much faster than Benjamin, as he had to hop along with his froggy hops, but he never lost sight of her lamp, until suddenly it moved to the right and disappeared.

Surprise caused Benjamin to stop in his tracks. He had never been this far from his pond before and the forest around him was dark, with only the moon for light. He could see tree branches, looking black and sinister as they moved in the breeze. Strange rustling sounds around him caused him to feel alone and afraid. Something furry brushed against him. "A-a-ah!!", he cried out. "I think I'll follow the path back to my safe familiar pond!"

He turned around, and a long dark shape lowered itself from one of the branches, and hung there in front of him.

"Oh no!" thought Benjamin, "A snake!" He tried to hop backwards away from it, but was so afraid that he couldn't move.

"Well well well – dinner," hissed the snake. "How convenient of you to hop by."

Benjamin gathered his courage and said as bravely as he could, "I'm on a mission for the Great King. You'd better not stop me!" At those words, the snake looked very afraid. It quickly slithered back to the branch on which it had been lying. Benjamin was very surprised. He hadn't expected that the name of the Great King would create such fear in the snake. As he hopped forward, he felt a strong comforting presence, as though he were no longer alone. He looked around, but could see no one.

He continued along the narrow path of Obedience,

until he came to the place where her light had veered to the right and when he looked, he saw that she stood waiting for him.

She turned and began to walk again. After he had hopped a little way, he looked up and discovered that he could no longer see the stars and treetops. He realized that this was because he had entered a cave, with a very high ceiling. Ahead of him the way took a bend to the left and he proceeded along around the corner, discovering himself in a brightly lit passage with high rock walls on each side. "I'm in a cave and I don't see any lamps. I wonder where the light is coming from," he thought.

As he was proceeding along the passageway, a group of animals passed him. There was a fox, a beaver and a dog, each of them full of energy and happiness. They nodded to Benjamin and smiled. Apparently they knew who he was and why he had come. "Woof! The king is waiting for you!" said the dog, and they bustled off.

After they had passed he turned to see, hovering next to him, a very bright light. It was only as big as he was himself and as he looked at it vibrating in the air, he realized that it was actually the glow from a little person, who was in the centre of the ball of light. She had huge eyes and tiny wings and seemed to constantly change colour. She was obviously very happy to see him. She clapped her hands, turned two summersaults and soared with a rush up towards the roof of the cavern, flying so high that Benjamin lost sight of her.

He looked ahead and saw that Obedience was standing at an opening of great height, which appeared to be the ending to the tunnel. She beckoned to him to follow her. Upon entering through the archway he found himself in a vast chamber with towering walls and a ceiling so high that he could hardly see it. He could smell the perfume of the beautiful vines and flowers that covered the walls. The flowers were of every colour and shade you could imagine, some bright and vibrant, some delicate and soft. "How do they bloom so brightly where there's no sun?" Benjamin wondered, "And how come this cavern is so bright? Where's the light coming from?"

Benjamin could see tables and chairs of all different shapes and sizes placed here and there on the floor of the cavern. A stream, crisscrossed by little bridges, splashed and gurgled its way from an opening on the opposite wall, passing where Benjamin was standing. As he watched, fish leapt exuberantly out of the water, some of them traveling an amazing distance through the air before plunging merrily into the laughing stream. These fascinating fish sparkled, their skin glittering as though each scale were a brightly coloured sequin. As they flew through the air, some winked and waved a fin at Benjamin. He was too astonished to wave back; he could only stand and stare. He had never seen fish behave like that on his pond.

The stream widened as it approached the wall to his left, where he saw a beautiful waterfall. Each droplet sparkled like a diamond with some colours Benjamin had never before seen. Benjamin looked at the waterfall, thinking that there was something strange about it, when all at once his eyes and mouth opened wide in astonishment, because he realized that the waterfall

wasn't going down into the river; it was going up from it! Benjamin lived on water, was well used to its ways and couldn't believe that he was looking at a waterfall going up instead of down. He didn't even know what to call it. "You can 't call it a waterfall if nothing's falling," he thought. As he watched the waters sparkle and dance their way to a height he could barely see, Benjamin felt a sense of great joy. It was as though his feelings were lifted with the water. He could hear each little droplet calling to him, "Be joyful! All's well! The king lives!"

Benjamin wondered about the source of power that caused the waters to rise to such a height.

On turning back towards the chamber, he could see more little creatures, some bustling to and fro carrying trays of food, and some just chatting and, like him, enjoying the flowers and the waters. They all glowed with a light that seemed to come from within, and yet was reflected from another source.

By this time, his guide had crossed the stream, using one of the bridges, and was standing at the same opening as that through which the stream was entering the cavern. Benjamin also crossed, now feeling no fear, and followed her as she disappeared under the high archway, walking alongside the sparkling stream.

CHAPTER 3

U pon emerging from the archway, Benjamin felt a breeze on his face. He looked up and discovered that he could once again see the stars. He found that he was in a walled grotto, with the same towering cliffs around him, covered with the same splendour as the walls in the chamber he had just left, the perfume of the flowers being wafted around by the gentle breeze.

He looked to his right and stopped in his tracks, staring at a person he immediately knew to be the Great King. Benjamin couldn't take his eyes away from him.

He sat on a magnificent golden throne, inlaid with jewels of all sizes and colours. They sparkled and glowed in the light, which Benjamin now realized was coming from the king himself. He wore royal robes of gold and purple, and a beautiful golden jewel-encrusted crown on his head. Benjamin also discovered the source of the river, as he saw that it flowed from underneath the throne on which the king sat, widening as it flowed along, with beautiful trees growing by its banks. There was a platform in front of the throne where he could receive and talk with his subjects.

Benjamin felt something tickle his side and realized that a friendly squirrel that didn't have his fluffy tail under control had scurried over to welcome him. Benjamin could hardly speak, as he was just a little frog and felt quite overwhelmed at the sight of this awesome person on the throne. One question did pop into his head, however, being a very wise practical frog,

"Where does everyone go when it rains?" he whispered

to the squirrel. His lovely guide looked on smiling, as the squirrel whispered in reply, "Oh it never rains here."

"Well then," continued Benjamin, still whispering, "How do the flowers and grasses get watered?"

"Oh," whispered the squirrel in reply, "a mist comes from the stream and waters all the growing things. I have a question for you," said the friendly squirrel, still in a whisper.

"What's that?" asked Benjamin, wondering what on earth the squirrel thought Benjamin could tell him.

"Why are we whispering?" whispered the squirrel.

"Because of the king – I thought we mustn't disturb him," explained Benjamin still in a whisper.

"Oh," said the squirrel in a normal tone of voice, "You don't have to worry about that. The king loves to hear our voices, especially when we are singing or talking to him."

Benjamin's eyes, already quite wide opened even wider in astonishment.

"That rich powerful king likes us to sing to him?" questioned Benjamin.

"Oh yes," the squirrel answered him. "He gave us the gift of music and he likes us to use it and give it back to him."

"All things come from him," said Obedience. "Come," she continued. "The king awaits."

CHAPTER 4

The king looked over at Benjamin, who found himself looking into smiling eyes full of kindness and encouragement. Obedience led him before the throne.

"Thank you, Obedience, for carrying out my instructions so faithfully." He then turned to the creatures assembled there. "Basil and Betty Badger, please make sure that Obedience is provided with something to eat and drink."

He turned to Benjamin. "Welcome little friend," he said. Benjamin felt quite taken aback by all this. "A king so greatly concerned for the welfare of his servant?" he thought "A king who called him friend?" He could only stare at the king speechlessly. He recovered his composure, remembering how he should behave before a king. He gave a low bow. The king nodded in acknowledgement and said to Benjamin, "You are a worthy servant; it took great courage to follow Obedience to this place."

Benjamin managed to find his tongue.

"Now that I am here, Your Majesty, I see that I need have had no fear. Everyone is so joyful in this kingdom."

The king again smiled and nodded, but a look of deep sadness crossed the king's face.

"There is something causing me great grief and that's why I have sent for you, my little loyal one." Benjamin felt very concerned that anything should cause this person to feel sad.

"I'll do anything I can to help you, your Majesty, but I'm just a little frog. How can I help a great king like you with your problems?"

"You have a willing heart, Benjamin," answered the king. "That's all I need, and your small size can be an asset; however, before I tell you of your mission, you must have rest and refreshment."

At the Great King's signal, two hedgehogs and one of the little glowing winged creatures he had seen in the cave came over. He could now see that the little person in the light was actually reflecting the light from the Great King.

"Come with us," said one of the hedgehogs. They led Benjamin to a table just the right size for him, already laden with all kinds of berries and fruit which, surprisingly, Benjamin found he had a real appetite for in this kingdom. After he had eaten his fill, they led him to a bed, again just the right size for him, in another chamber. Benjamin didn't think he could possibly sleep, after all that had happened to him, but once lying in the extremely comfortable bed and feeling very safe in the realm of this awesome king, and very tired after hopping such a long way, he found himself drifting off to sleep, lulled by the sweet music he could hear as everyone sang to their beloved king.

CHAPTER 5

U pon awakening from a very refreshing sleep, Benjamin saw Obedience waiting close by.

"Is the king awake?" he asked.

"The king never sleeps," answered Obedience. This puzzled Benjamin immensely, but so did many things in this very strange kingdom.

Having followed Obedience back to the throne, Benjamin bowed before the king, who, looking very serious bid him rise.

"There is another kingdom in this realm, Benjamin," he began to explain, "not at all like this one. There, a creature called Wickedness reigns with his two servants, Temptation and Deceit. Three of my children have wandered away into that kingdom, lured by the lies and tricks of Deceit and have been captured and imprisoned by Wickedness. I need someone with a loyal heart, willing to follow Obedience to go down into this dark kingdom and rescue my children and lead them back to me." Benjamin looked very afraid at this. On seeing his fear, the king reached out and placed a hand on his head, continuing, "Remember, Benjamin, I will always be with you. Even when you can't see me, I am still there. Your small size, which you see as a weakness, I know will give you an advantage in many situations."

"But Majesty," Benjamin ventured to ask, "If you will be there anyway, why don't you do this yourself?"

"Because I choose to allow you to perform this task, otherwise you could not know me, and I could not reward you," answered the Great King. Benjamin still looked very puzzled. The king only smiled a smile of great kindness and understanding, but would not answer his question more fully.

"I will not allow you to go into the battle unequipped. When I ask one of my servants to perform a service, or fight a battle, I always provide them with whatever will be needed to perform the task."

With that, the king nodded to a little beaver who seemed to be always busy. Benjamin thought of the busy beaver family back in his own pond, and decided that all beavers must be pretty much the same, no matter where you might meet them.

The beaver left with two others and they came back carrying what looked to Benjamin like a suit of armour.

Buster Beaver brought a shining silver helmet and a strong breastplate made of the same material as the helmet. Basil Beaver took the helmet and placed it on Benjamin's head. "This helmet," said the Great King, "will protect not only your head, but also your thoughts. You will not be easily tricked by Deceit and Temptation. It will help you remember your meeting with me and your becoming my friend and joining my service, also that I am with you and trusting you."

Basil Beaver then fastened the breastplate on Benjamin's chest. "This breastplate will protect your heart from the arrows and thrusts of Temptation and remind you that you are in the service of the Great King.

Bobby Beaver handed Benjamin a pair of strong leather boots. As Benjamin put them on, the king said, "These boots will help guide your feet in following Obedience as she leads you through the kingdom of

Wickedness. They will help you to stand firm against Deceit and Temptation."

After Benjamin had finished putting on the boots, Bobby Beaver buckled a belt around Benjamin's waist. "The belt," the king informed Benjamin, "will protect you from the arrows of Deceit and help you know truth."

The third beaver, Billy, had brought a shield and a sword. He handed the shield to Benjamin and the king instructed him, "Never let this shield be taken from your hand. The enemy will shoot fiery darts and arrows at you. As long as you face them and hold up the shield, you will be safe." As the king handed it over, Benjamin looked at it. It was glowing with the same reflected light as the rest of the armour. On the shield there was the image of a lion wearing a crown emblazoned with jewels. The eyes of the lion were of stones more beautiful than diamonds. The strange thing was that as Benjamin looked at the lion, it seemed to look back at him as though it were alive. Its eyes appeared to Benjamin to have an expression very like those of the king – one of great understanding and encouragement, but also great courage. As Benjamin stared, those eyes grew fierce and terrible and he could see the fire deep within the stones. Benjamin almost dropped the shield in fright, but he remembered the words of the king "Do not let this shield out of your hand, Benjamin." Although he felt afraid, he trusted the king and held on tightly to the shield.

"Excellent, my loyal stalwart servant. I saw your fear but you need never be afraid of the lion. His anger is never directed at my friends; only at my enemies, for my enemies are also yours. Keep the shield facing them and you will never be alone."

The feeling of joy he experienced when wearing the armour was much greater than that afforded by even his favourite lily pad. Benjamin decided that he would not have wanted to miss these new sensations for anything and although he didn't know what would happen, for this moment, was glad he had come on this great adventure.

Billy then handed Benjamin a beautiful two-edged sword. The handle was in the shape of a cross, glowing with rubies. The sword shone brightly, at first almost blinding Benjamin, but as he looked at the blade of the sword, he began to see himself very clearly. "You need never be afraid to look upon this sword, Benjamin," the king assured him, "because you have a good heart. However, anyone at whom you point the sword sees himself or herself as they really are." After saying these words, the king stood up from his throne, and his voice became very powerful, bearing in it the ring of victory. His eyes became intense, glowing and piercing as the lion's eyes.

"The sword has the power to pierce the soul and to break or heal the heart. It will cut away misery and destroy evil!" As Benjamin listened and watched him, he realized that this was a very mighty, powerful person. Benjamin knew that this was a king totally kind and loving to his followers, but also avenging and terrible in the face of evil. Benjamin was also very puzzled. "How can a sword do all that, Your Majesty?" The Great King said only "These things will be revealed at the right time."

One of the beavers then produced a slingshot and a bag of rocks and tucked them into Benjamin's belt.

The king looked very seriously at Benjamin for several moments and then a slow smile began to cross his face.

"I give you Godspeed, little friend. Always remember, you will never be alone. You have the lion always with you. Always follow the path of Obedience."

Obedience then came forward. For the first time Benjamin saw her looking sad.

"I do not wish to go into that kingdom, Majesty," she told the king.

"I am aware of that, faithful servant," said the king, "but I have need of your service there." He lifted Obedience's lantern from where she had laid it beside the throne, and immediately it once again glowed with the light, which came from the king.

"Why does she need a lantern?" asked Benjamin, "Your light is everywhere in the Kingdom"

"You are entering the kingdom of darkness," responded the king. "My light is not there unless Obedience carries it there."

The king once again looked at Obedience and handed her the lantern. "I need you to carry my light into the darkness and lead the way, Obedience."

"Then I will go, my Lord."

"I know you will, Obedience, my courageous, always faithful one."

Benjamin could see that there was a great love between the Great King and Obedience.

The king then pointed out from the throne towards

the other end of the grotto. Benjamin had hardly looked there, since his attention had been taken up so much with the king. When Benjamin turned, he could see that the river had several tributaries, which flowed into the openings of several caves. Obedience stepped from the platform and began walking alongside one of the streams towards an extremely high, dark opening.

CHAPTER 6

All the king's subjects were present and had lined up alongside the stream. As Benjamin walked along, once again following Obedience, they reached out and patted him, wishing him well and encouraging him. This really helped him, as the sight of this great dark cavern was causing him to feel afraid. Benjamin turned and looked at the Great King who was still pointing, standing very great and powerful, now shining with a light almost blinding to Benjamin. The little frog stood feasting his eyes for a few moments, as he wanted to carry the memory of the Great King's light and power into the darkness. He then turned and stepped into the cave.

Obedience led Benjamin deep into the dark cave. The path began to slope downward. "Brr, it's cold and getting colder," he thought. When he looked back, he could no longer see the bright land of the Great king. He became aware of scuttling, scraping noises and realized that they were not alone in the cave. He peered carefully around, trying to pierce the gloom. He could see creatures, some his own size and some larger, moving around him, but keeping their distance. They seemed to be afraid, and he realized that they were afraid not only of him, but especially of the shield he was carrying. He held it up in front of him, letting it cover most of his body. The creatures he could see in this cave were nothing like the ones in the kingdom of the Great king. They were ugly, with no light shining from them. Some had been wounded in a previous battle and were unable to walk properly. There was no joy here, only darkness, cold and fear.

"I don't like this place," he thought. "I'm going to return to the kingdom of light and joy."

With these rebellious thoughts, he looked ahead and realized that he had lost sight of Obedience. He felt even more afraid, remembering the same experience in the forest. While he stood there, unable to move from fear, six of the ugly creatures surrounded him and began jabbing at him with swords and sharp sticks. He panicked. "Help me someone!" he shouted. He tried to run away, but the creatures wouldn't allow him to. "I'm just going to have to stand and fight!" He decided.

He drew his sword. Immediately the words of the Great King came to him. "You will never be alone; I will be there. The shield will protect you!" That was when he realized he had dropped his shield. The ugly creatures were trying to drive him away from it, but he called out "Help me Great King!" When they heard Benjamin calling to the king, the creatures hesitated and he took advantage of this to use his sword to push their weapons up and away from him. He darted under them to grab the shield. The creatures surrounding him lunged at him as he ducked, and instead jabbed and wounded each other.

Strength and courage began to flow through his veins, and he could feel that invisible presence which he had felt in the forest. He picked up the shield and holding it, pointed his sword at the enemy. The creatures darted back, covering their ears and closing their eyes. "They're deafened by the sword! They can't bear to look at it!" cried Benjamin. "They're seeing their reflections in the sword and can see themselves as evil and ugly as they really are!"

The creatures couldn't bear the sight and turned away, covering their eyes. "We remember his words! The words of the Great King!" One creature, after staring at the shield, turned and ran in terror. The others slunk away, moaning in great sadness and fear.

As he watched them go, Benjamin thought, "I didn't strike a blow! All I did was hold up the king's weapons, and stand to face the enemy. The king's weapons won the battle!"

Benjamin turned and saw Obedience ahead of him and began, once again, to follow her path, still aware of the strength within him. He thought of his new friend the Great King and felt very grateful to him for the armour to deal with the enemy. He touched the sword, which was once again in his belt, and he thought he could hear the king's voice saying, "I will always be with you, Benjamin. You fought the battle well, my valiant little friend."

Benjamin found himself replying, "But I didn't really do anything, Your Majesty."

"You did all that was required of you," came the reply. Benjamin thought it rather strange to find himself carrying on a conversation with someone he couldn't see. "Oh well," he thought, "that's just one more strange thing about this adventure."

As he walked along, he began to hear a deep rumbling noise. Ahead of him the cave took a bend to the right and he very slowly and carefully peeped around the corner.

CHAPTER 7

U p ahead he saw a pair of high gates of very thick black metal bars, with a large lock. The gates took up the whole breadth of the cave, stretching across the river, which still flowed down the centre of the cave. He couldn't see whether they reached right up to the ceiling, because he couldn't see the ceiling, but they went to a great height. Beyond the gates he could hear yelling, banging and rattling. He could also hear sobbing.

It was not so dark beyond this point, because every so often along the wall there was a lamp burning. It was still very gloomy, but Benjamin could see that on the other side of the gate, at each end of it stood two huge creatures – much larger than the ones he had already met, each armed with an enormous sword and a heavy spear. They also had a large key, obviously for the gate. Both creatures were asleep, one actually snoring, which accounted for the rumbling noise he had heard. Benjamin began to approach the gates stealthily. As he drew closer, he realized that he could squeeze through between the bars, without having to unlock the gate. He touched the sword at his side for reassurance and understood the king's words "Your small size can be an asset."

Benjamin began to move quietly forward. He hopped through the gate, passing between the bars and the two creatures, noticing that in height, he reached not much higher than their ankles. As he passed them, one of the creatures began to wake up, stretching, snorting and groaning loudly. At this, Benjamin panicked and began to hop away as fast as he could. As he did so, his sword hit the ground, making a clanking, scraping sound. The

ugly guard heard it, looked down and saw Benjamin. He roared loudly, waking his companion. Benjamin tried to hop even faster but realized he couldn't outrun his huge enemy and the weapons the Great King had given him did not protect his back. He remembered the words of the king, "I will never leave you." He turned around to face his pursuers and called to the king for help. "Oh Great King, I am in much trouble!" When the guards heard the name of the king called out, they stopped in their track and began to quake in fear. They saw his shield, and as they looked at it, it took on a life of its own. Benjamin felt it shake and a terrible roar of the lion filled the cavern. All of a sudden, the great lion leapt from the shield and held one of the creatures at bay, but didn't fight it.

Benjamin was small and was able to avoid the lunges of the other giant, at the same time jabbing at the creature's feet and ankles with the sword. As he did this, the creature kept losing strength and was using the wall to remain upright. Benjamin remembered the sling and rocks the Great King had given him. He put a stone into the slingshot and aimed at the giant. He hit him right in the middle of the forehead. With a great crash, the giant fell dead. The other creature was so afraid, that it ran into the entrance of a tunnel and fled.

"Give me the key Benjamin," said Obedience. Benjamin took the key from the belt of the huge creature. It was a large key, and Benjamin had trouble handling it, but he half dragged, half carried the key to Obedience. She took it from him and brought it through the bars, opened the gates and stepped through, relocking it behind her. "That will stop anyone from following us," she said.

Benjamin was full of confidence, now, and said to Obedience and the lion, "I'm going after the one that ran away."

"No", said Obedience. "That isn't the quest the Great King sent you on. You must now continue to follow my path." Benjamin ignored her and ran into the tunnel, after the creature.

As he progressed into the tunnel, he no longer had the

light of Obedience to follow, and it became very dark. He dropped his sword, and couldn't find it in the darkness. Suddenly he heard the creature coming back. He felt very afraid because he had dropped his weapon, and the giant knew he was afraid. It laughed and came towards Benjamin.

"I should have remembered that I was fighting with the weapons of the king, and not on my own strength. I wish I had listened to Obedience and not stubbornly gone my own way."

No sooner had he thought this than a light appeared and he could once again see his sword. He also noticed that his armour had become dull and had patches of mud. His feet had changed colour and were becoming the same colour as the giant. He grabbed his sword and began fighting the giant, but his movements were slower and he couldn't stay away from the enemy's attacks. Suddenly, the giant aimed his foot at Benjamin and knocked him rolling along the ground. He managed to get up, but he had hurt his hip. He felt weak and was bleeding and covered with the mud of the Kingdom of Wickedness. He had little strength left to fight and felt discouragement and fear as he saw the creature approaching. As it bent towards him, Benjamin in desperation threw his sword and struck the giant in the chest, killing him.

Benjamin struggled to his feet, took his sword and turned to go back the way he had come. To his surprise and relief, he saw Obedience waiting for him. He realized it had been her light that had enabled him to find his sword. He slowly limped towards her.

"I've ruined everything, now. I can't help the children of the Great King feeling like this."

"You haven't ruined everything. You wandered away from my path, but you're back on it now. Go and wash in the River of Living Water. You'll feel much better."

Benjamin limped towards the river and lowered himself into the water. Some fish came to help him, bathing his wounds and washing his armour. Soon Benjamin felt much better, but as he stepped from the water and began to walk, he realized that his hip was still painful.

"I feel better, but my hip still hurts."

"Yes," said Obedience, "There's always a consequence when you wander away from my path."

"You are indeed a good servant of the Great King, Obedience. He is right to trust you. I keep wanting to do things my way and prove how great I am, rather than remembering that all things come from him."

"You are learning step by step, Benjamin. You are still on the quest the Great King has given you. You haven't turned back. That's what he asks of you."

"Yes, everything the Great King said was true."

CHAPTER 8

The two traveled on, following the stream. The cavern floor took on a steeper downwards slope. Some of the ugly creatures passed him, going in the opposite direction, their eyes full of sadness and fear. There was a foul smell coming from them, which became stronger the more deeply they descended into the kingdom of Wickedness.

Upon rounding a bend, he could see the end of the tunnel. Here the smell was almost unbearable. He could hear arguing and fighting, as well as moaning and sobbing. He carefully peeped around the opening and saw that he had come to a larger room. At the far end on a great, dark throne, sat a person who looked quite handsome, yet Benjamin realized that he was the source of the stench, which rubbed on to his followers. He was tall and powerful looking, with broad shoulders. He was dressed in black and carried a sword at his side. He had a frown on his face and smiled at no-one.

"Who is that?" questioned Benjamin

"That's Wickedness, the ruler of this kingdom," answered Obedience.

"I expected him to look ugly, like his followers."

"He is. What you are seeing is a deception," answered Obedience.

The stream of the Great King flowed across the room, making its way below a cage containing three children.

"Those are the children of the Great King," Obedience told him.

"The ones I am to rescue?" said Benjamin.

"Yes," answered Obedience.

To Benjamin's horror, he saw that they had begun to change. The smell of Wickedness was on them, and they were beginning to take on the physical appearance of the followers of Wickedness.

As the water from the stream swept under the cage, some droplets splashed on to the three children. Benjamin noticed that the parts most often touched by the water, especially their feet, were the parts least affected by the Kingdom of Wickedness. The water was protecting them, not allowing the wickedness to completely take them over. Wickedness, on his throne was watching this and was angry at the saving power of the river.

"Move the cage!" he roared to one of his soldiers. No matter how hard they tried, however, they couldn't budge it. As they were struggling with the cage, the water was splashing them. Two of them jumped back, but one, who bore a slight resemblance to the children, seemed to like it. He was about to put his fingers in the water when Wickedness bellowed, "Take him away from the river!" Immediately the other two guards pulled him back, dragging him away from the Great King's stream.

"I hate that river!" bellowed Wickedness. " No matter where I make my throne room, the river changes course and is there! I can't escape from its presence!"

Benjamin noticed an increase in the smell and suddenly felt himself lifted into the air. He recoiled in disgust, not wanting anything from this kingdom to touch him or rub off onto him. He was being held by one of the creatures of Wickedness.

CHAPTER 9

B enjamin didn't panic this time. He had experienced the power of the Great King enough to know that even in this throne room, his power was greater than anything Benjamin might encounter.

"Well, well, what have we here?" said the huge creature holding Benjamin. He actually looked quite friendly, and wasn't nearly as ugly as the others in that kingdom. He was tall and slender, wearing a green top, blue tights and black shoes. He looked like a person whom the Kingdom of Wickedness had barely touched – except for the smell coming from him. He also was wearing a sword at his side. His attitude was friendly. He smiled at Benjamin – but the smile didn't reach his eyes.

"Have you left the kingdom of light? Why don't you join us? You can have anything you want, so long as you give your loyalty to our generous king, who sits on the throne. He will give you anything you want." As he said this, with a peculiar hiss in his voice, he pointed towards Wickedness who was at that moment still scowling at the river and the cage of the Great King's children and who hadn't yet noticed Benjamin.

"You will never want for anything," continued the creature, "You can have as much food as you want. We have a very good time here. There are no rules, unlike the kingdom you have just left. You can do anything you want here!"

"Who are you?" asked Benjamin, in a bold voice.

"My name is Temptation," answered the creature. "I have helped many people escape from the other kingdom.

I am King Wickedness' first Lieutenant. If you stay here, I will always be close at hand to lead and guide you!"

"NO!" yelled Benjamin. He drew his sword and poked his huge enemy with it, and shouted, "Hail to the Great King!" Temptation let go of Benjamin to cover his ears. Temptation then also drew his sword and tried to hit Benjamin on the head or pierce him in the heart, but Benjamin's breastplate and helmet protected him from the thrusts of Temptation. Benjamin remembered the words of the Great King "Do not let go of the shield! Never turn your back on the enemy!

Benjamin called out, "In the name of the Great King, I know he is more powerful than all the powers of Wickedness. He will help me now!"

As Temptation attacked him, Benjamin raised his shield. Once again he heard the lion's roar. He kept jabbing at Temptation wherever he could reach, and dodging about. He was so little that Temptation couldn't catch him with his sword and was becoming more and more angry and frustrated, particularly since Benjamin, after every few jabs kept calling out, "Hail to the Great King!" He held up the sword for one more jab. Temptation caught sight of his reflection in the sword; only his eyes, but that was enough. He stopped fighting in shock for long enough to allow Benjamin to throw the sword at his chest. The sword struck the heart of Temptation and he fell dead.

Obedience had not yet entered the throne room; she was still standing out of sight in the entrance. Benjamin hopped to where she could hear him.

"Obedience, I need you to distract Wickedness! I see a key which might open the cage!" With that, Obedience stepped into the room, swinging her lantern, singing a favourite song of the Great King. Wickedness looked at her, astonished. "My warning systems have been rendered useless by a crazy woman! Where are the guards at the gates?!! Why was I not told we have intruders? Why are you all just standing there?! Take her! Get Deceit in here!!"

At this, a great roar shook the whole room, and the lion leapt from Benjamin's shield, to stand between Wickedness' creatures and Obedience.

Benjamin, meantime, had slipped beside the throne of Wickedness and standing on a cushion reached up with his sword and unhooked the key hanging there. It was a very unusual key, being made of gold with words written down the sides in a strange language. Here is what the inscription looked like:

Down one side:
M X V W L F H
I R U J L Y H Q H V V

Down the other side:
W K H J U H D M N L Q J

Benjamin also noticed a roll of parchment hanging beside the key, and he took that off, also. He slipped behind the throne an unrolled it. It was clues to the solution of the coded message. If you look on the page 72, you will see clues to solve the coded message.

Benjamin rolled the scrolls up again and used his slingshot to fire them and the key to Obedience.

Benjamin then poked Wickedness in the ankle with his sword. Wickedness, furious, turned his attention to Benjamin, stood up and tried to kick him. Benjamin dodged around, jabbing at Wickedness.

Obedience, still accompanied by the lion, walked across one of the bridges over the river and began to walk towards the chain which, tied to a hook on the wall, held the cage suspended over the river. She unwound it and lowered the cage until it came to rest spanning the river, each end sitting on an opposite bank. She then ran back to the side of the river on which Benjamin was fighting Wickedness and she unlocked the cage, allowing the three children to escape. She pointed to the exit from the throne room and the three children, after drinking from the River of Life, ran to the exit.

Benjamin, meantime, was continuing his fight with Wickedness, calling out "In the name of the Great King!" and "Praise the the king of the Kingdom of Light!" Wickedness was becoming more and more furious and frustrated at not being able to kill and silence Benjamin who, taking a high froggy leap, caught hold of Wickedness' belt, one end of which was hanging down just above Wickedness' knee, and Benjamin began to poke him around the thigh just above the knee. Wickedness tried to catch Benjamin, but couldn't. Once he aimed his sword at Benjamin, but Benjamin dodged the sword and Wickedness pierced himself instead. Benjamin leapt down to the ground and began the fight anew there. Wickedness was backing away from Benjamin, trying to keep him from continually jabbing his ankles. Benjamin kept moving forward, backing Wickedness towards the cage, which sat with the door still open. Benjamin suddenly leapt around behind Wickedness and began jabbing at the creature's ankles from behind. Wickedness gave a twist around to try to catch Benjamin, lost his balance gave a great roar, and fell into the cage.

"In the name of the Great King!" cried Benjamin while he and Obedience slammed the cage door shut, and Obedience locked it.

"Well done, brave Obedience!" cried Benjamin, dancing a figure eight jig around Obedience, waving his sword in circles in the air.

"Careful, Benjamin!" she said, "I don't want to be jabbed!"

"Never, my lady!" replied Benjamin, ending the dance with a deep bow.

While Wickedness roared in fury at being trapped in the cage, Benjamin looked around and saw a witch come into the room.

CHAPTER 10

"What is your name?" asked Benjamin.

"My name is Deceit," she cackled. He realized that this was another of Wickedness' lieutenants. She came slowly towards the little frog, smiling at him.

"Well, my little toad, you're in a very sorry position, aren't you?" Benjamin was quite taken aback by this statement. It seemed to him that they were the ones who should be worried, and not he. "The Great King really has you deceived, hasn't he?" Here Benjamin made the mistake of speaking with her.

"In what way?" he asked.

"Well, you think he's so good and powerful, but he's really lying to you." As she spoke, she was slowly moving closer to Benjamin, while unnoticed by him, a creature under Deceit's command was unbuckling the belt around Benjamin's waist.

"The lion has left the shield. It's no longer there," screeched Deceit. "The king has brought you to this kingdom only to abandon you. He really doesn't care about you or his children. They were trying to escape from him. He's not really who he says he is, and he has very little power."

Benjamin was staring into the eyes of Deceit, listening to her. She seemed to weave a spell around him. Deceit reached out her hand to him. "Come," she whispered, "You don't need him. This kingdom has the true king. He cares for your pleasure. Join us in the Kingdom of Wickedness."

By this time, the belt of truth the Great King had

given Benjamin was no longer around his waist. He could no longer feel the life in the shield and was beginning to feel afraid as he was listening to her lies. Deceit then made a signal and a dozen creatures behind him aimed their flaming arrows at him. Benjamin took a leap backwards as Deceit was moving closer and almost fell over the belt lying on the floor. This brought him out of the daze Deceit had brought upon him, and he raised the sword, sensing danger. The king's words came back to him, "I will never leave you. The belt will protect you from the lies of Deceit."

Deceit made another signal to the creatures behind Benjamin just as he bent to put down his sword and pick up the belt. The creatures behind him fired their arrows in response to Deceit's signal. They went right over Benjamin, causing Deceit to jump around dodging the arrows of her own troops. Benjamin managed to put on the belt and pick up the sword as this was going on. The power of Deceit was immediately broken. 'You are well named!" he said. "You are full of lies and deceit." Deceit cowered, turning away from the sword. Benjamin leapt around her, jabbing the sword at her. Her troops gathered around, trying to help her. They all tried to catch Benjamin who used his shield to protect himself as he leapt around Deceit. All they accomplished was total confusion as they pushed and fell over each other. Deceit was desperately trying to avoid looking at the sword, but finally caught sight of her reflection and could no longer turn away. She was caught in the sight of her own wickedness and began to shrink. She struggled to escape from the sword, but was unable to do so. She screamed for help, but none came, and she gradually shrunk away into nothingness. Deceit had been wiped out by the truth of the sword.

Suddenly there was a loud rumbling sound and Benjamin felt the ground beneath his feet shake. He turned around to see an amazing thing happening to the throne of Wickedness.

CHAPTER 11

Benjamin stared in amazement as the ground beneath the throne opened up and the throne toppled into the newly formed hole. Wickedness, still in the cage, roared with rage and began doubling his efforts to escape from the cage. He kicked against the bars and shook them and tried to force open the cage door, but to no avail. He was held fast. The ground continued to shake causing the cage to begin to tip.

"Help me push it over, Obedience," yelled Benjamin, and together they pushed on the cage until it fell with a crash on to its side, with Wickedness still inside. "Let's roll it!" cried Benjamin. The children saw what was happening and ran to help. Together, helped by the heaving of the ground, they caused the cage to roll towards the hole into which the throne had fallen. Finally, they came to the edge and gave one last push, and the cage and Wickedness fell into the hole.

Benjamin began hopping all over the place, waving his sword in the air. "In the name of the Great King!" he yelled, totally excited and delighted at the amazing turn of events. All of a sudden, more creatures came rushing, shouting for joy, into the room and leapt into the River of Life, cleansing themselves of the ugliness with which Wickedness had covered them, while other uglier creatures, enraged, tried to stop them. Benjamin ran to any of them who were holding a creature back and jabbed at them with his sword, yelling, "Hail to the powerful Great King!" The lion roared at others, and they let go in fear.

Benjamin saw two of the creatures having an argument.

After watching for a minute, he turned to Obedience and asked, "Do you know their names?"

"Yes," answered Obedience, "The smaller one is Pliable and the larger is Discouragement."

As Benjamin watched, he heard Pliable say, "I want to jump into the River of Life. I want to go into the Kingdom of the Great King! What do you think, Discouragement?"

"Don't be silly, Pliable," answered Discouragement, pulling him away from the river. "You're too ugly. He wouldn't want you. You'd hate it there. You'd be really unhappy." Benjamin watched as Pliable turned sadly away from the river, led by Discouragement. Benjamin began jumping up and down waving his arms at Pliable and pointing at the river and shouting, "Yes, yes, come into our kingdom! There's lots of room! The Great King will want you there!" As Pliable turned once more towards the river, Discouragement once again pulled him back, saying, "Don't listen to the frog. What does he know?"

"I know that if you don't leave Pliable alone, I'll jab you with my sword and send you hopping!" True to his word, Benjamin drew his sword, ran at Discouragement, and began poking him with his sword. Discouragement turned and ran, loosing his grip on Pliable. Benjamin pointed his sword at the river and nodded at Pliable. The Lion gave an encouraging roar, and Pliable ran to the river and jumped in. The mud and filth of Wickedness began to wash off and Pliable jumped and splashed in the river, filled with joy. Some of the brightly coloured fish came to share in the fun, swimming and leaping around Pliable. Benjamin hopped and danced about yelling "Another one for the Kingdom of the Great King!" He watched as Pliable climbed out on to the opposite bank and joined the creatures already waiting. He looked more like a citizen of the Kingdom of Light, than of that dark kingdom. "Yes!!" called Benjamin, raising both arms in the air and hopping around in delight.

This continued for some time, with more and more of the inhabitants of the kingdom of Wickedness leaping into the river and climbing out on to the opposite bank. When no one else was leaping in, Benjamin was about to jump in and cross, himself, when he heard a strange shuffling noise coming from the tunnel behind those who had not chosen freedom from Wickedness. Benjamin watched as there appeared at the mouth of the tunnel, a creature who had been imprisoned by Wickedness for so long that his body was extremely twisted and he could no longer even walk properly. "That's Depravity," Obedience told Benjamin. "He was a favourite of Wickedness." He was partly crawling and sometimes dragging himself along the ground, finally collapsing in exhaustion before he could reach the river. The other creatures laughed and jeered at him, some even poking him with their sharp claws, saying things like, "Not so great now, are you, Depravity?'

Much to Benjamin's surprise, he saw a lamb crossing one of the bridges and walk towards Depravity. He could see blood on the lamb's side. "Look," he said to Obedience, "there's a lamb, and it's been wounded." The lamb walked up to Depravity and lay down beside him, touched one of Depravity's hands with its hoof, and whispered to him.

Depravity began to weep and once again tried to reach the river, but couldn't raise himself. Obedience went to help him and she and the lamb lifted him on to the lion's back. The lion jumped into the river and swam to the middle, carrying Depravity. Benjamin leapt in and joined them, and the fish came and washed Depravity, while the lion helped him stand. Benjamin swam and hopped around, encouraging everyone. Gradually, as the filth of Wickedness was washed from Depravity, he stood on his own and began to help cleanse himself. Finally, he smiled.

"Thank you so much," he said to everyone.

"No," answered Benjamin, "Don't thank us, thank The Great King."

"Where is he?" asked Depravity.

"Don't worry," said Benjamin, "You'll see him soon."

"Oh," said Depravity, pointing. "He needs help." Benjamin looked around and saw a very small creature trying to climb from the river. "I'll give him a hand," said Depravity, and with that, he walked along the edge of the river and took the hand of a very frustrated very small person who was trying to climb out from the river. Benjamin watched as Depravity took the little man on his shoulder and headed for the gathering of creatures waiting on the banks of the River of Life.

Benjamin looked around. "Where did the lamb go?" he asked Obedience.

"Back to the Kingdom of Light," she answered.

The lion climbed from the river and shook himself. From his mane and his body danced a million drops of water, shining and sparkling like diamonds.

The lion then gave a great roar, which shook the cavern. "It's still shaking," Benjamin said to Obedience, "even though the lion is no longer roaring."

"Quickly," she told Benjamin, "Go to the front of the line, and lead them to the exit. There's no time to lose!"

Benjamin now knew better than to argue with Obedience, and immediately followed her instructions, hopping along, losing no time in heading for the front of the line.

"Follow the frog!" Obedience called to everyone. As she was saying this, the cavern was beginning to shake more violently.

CHAPTER 12

M any of the creatures began to panic as they heard rumbling and felt shaking.

Obedience and the three children ran up and down the long line reassuring and hurrying the creatures.

"It's OK!" Obedience was calling, "Don't panic. Just don't waste any time in leaving!"

"Don't be afraid! Our Dad's waiting for us!" the children were saying. "You'll be OK, but hurry, hurry!"

Benjamin led them to the tunnel through which he had entered the cavern, with the three children of the Great King walking behind him, followed by hundreds of the joyful creatures, shining and beautiful, rescued from the Kingdom of Wickedness. Just before Benjamin stepped into the tunnel, he looked back towards the pit where Wickedness was imprisoned, just in time to see a huge piece of rock fall from the ceiling into the pit, completely blocking it up.

Once in the tunnel, Obedience took the lead, going on ahead, her light shining in the darkness to show the way back to the Great King. As the last of the freed creatures stepped into the tunnel, the whole ceiling of Wickedness' throne room began to collapse, closing up the tunnels and destroying the kingdom of Wickedness, burying the remaining inhabitants with their chosen king. He saw no rocks fall into the river of the Great King, however, which continued to flow, and could never be stopped.

As the long procession made its way through the tunnel, led by the light of Obedience, they could hear rumbling behind them as the parts of the tunnel through which they had just passed began to collapse. They came to the huge gates where Benjamin had fought the giants, but the two giants were, of course, no longer there. Obedience unlocked the gates with the key she still carried, and everyone passed through safely and continued the journey up towards the Kingdom of Light.

As they approached the exit from the tunnel, some of the creatures Benjamin had met at the beginning of his journey once again scuttled up to him ready to do battle. Benjamin felt no fear, as he faced them, drawing his sword. Two of the attackers approached him. He held up his shield and waved his sword in an arc. "For the Great King!" he cried. He clashed swords with the two creatures, but they were no match for him. One of them ran back farther into the tunnel, but the other stayed to fight. He wasn't much bigger than Benjamin so they clashed swords. Benjamin was fighting hard, and backing his opponent farther into the tunnel. The creature realized that he couldn't defeat Benjamin and turned and ran farther into the tunnel. Benjamin was about to give chase, but Obedience called, "Benjamin, finish your quest. We can't stay here. The tunnel is collapsing."

"You are right as always, Obedience. We must proceed." He once again took his place at the head of the procession, and moved forward.

Finally, they emerged into the Kingdom of the Great King, Obedience first, followed by Benjamin and the king's three children, and then all the creatures who had chosen to depart from Wickedness.

The king's subjects of many different types, many of which Benjamin had never seen before, had formed two lines which stretched from the entrance of the tunnel to the throne. Benjamin and Obedience and the whole procession passed along between these lines as they walked towards the throne. The whole kingdom was singing and dancing and celebrating the escape from the dark kingdom.

The king was happiest of all. He was standing before his throne, with his arms open, waiting to receive his children. They ran to him and he took them up in his arms, laughing and crying at the same time. He then turned to Benjamin and took him into his arms. Benjamin couldn't believe that this Great King was actually hugging him. Obedience smiled happily, as she watched the king embrace him.

The Great King then asked all those who had been rescued from the kingdom of Wickedness to come forward. They fell silent, thinking that the King would be angry with them for entering the enemy's kingdom. They were expecting punishment. Instead, as each of his restored subjects came forward, he opened his arms and held them in a big hug, welcoming each personally back into his kingdom, and giving each of them a new name.

As Depravity stepped up, Benjamin watched as the king looked seriously at Depravity, who fell on his knees before the Great King.

"Great King, I am guilty of many things, before and after I entered the Kingdom of Wickedness. I ignored the ones you sent to warn me and pull me back towards you, and listened instead to Temptation and Deceit, the two lieutenants of Wickedness. They made Wickedness seem so much fun, and at first it was, but the longer I stayed in the Kingdom of Wickedness, the more it became miserable and without love or trust or friendship. I beg for your forgiveness, and vow that if you will allow me to stay in your Kingdom, you will not find a more loyal, trustworthy servant in all of your Kingdom."

Benjamin stepped up before the throne, and said "Sire, I would speak for Depravity. He put up a great struggle to reach the River of Life, and left it a cleansed, joyful creature. I saw him help some others climb out of the river and encourage them."

"Thank you, Benjamin for those words," said Depravity.

The Great King reached out to Depravity, and said to him, "Stand. Your name is no longer Depravity. It is now Glowing One." The Great King picked up a small rock and wrote a name on it. He handed it to Glowing One. "I have written your name "Glowing One" on this rock. If you ever think back to what you were in the Kingdom of Wickedness and feel guilty, look at this rock and it will remind you of what you are now, in my eyes. You are now Glowing One. You will be in my service as one of my trusted messengers."

Tears ran down the face of Glowing one. "Thank you, Majesty. You will find me trustworthy and obedient."

"I know that, Glowing One."

Next was Pliable. The Great King smiled at him. "What do you wish, Pliable?" said the King.

"Majesty, I wish to sit at your feet and learn of you. I

want to be strong, able to know the truth and stay strong and fight for it."

"Your name is no longer Pliable, but Decisive, because that is what you will become. Yes, you may sit at my feet and learn about this kingdom and about truth so that you will know what is right and stand by it." Decisive immediately stepped over and sat on the step beside the throne of The Great King. One of the little beavers brought him a cushion.

The Great King then said to Benjamin, "You must be hungry, my valiant friend." He then turned to his servants. "Bring in the feast"

CHAPTER 13

At the King's command, tables in the next room were moved together and a great bustling began, with talking and laughing servants carrying plates laden with all kinds of fruit, vegetables, desserts, drinks and flowers for the tables. The fish leapt higher from the water, which gurgled even more merrily and sparkled more brightly than ever.

What a feast and celebration they had. Glowing One and Decisive came to bring Benjamin to the feast. He rode to the Feast on Glowing One's shoulder.

"Seat him at my table," instructed the King. Benjamin was seated at the king's table with Obedience and the three children. He was no longer in his armour, which had been removed and carried off by the ever-busy beavers. Benjamin had been especially sorry to part with the shield and the sword, which he had come to think of as special friends.

After the feast, the king stood up. "My heart is full," he said. "My children whom I had lost have been restored to me." He turned to Benjamin. "You were brave and stalwart, my friend, and now you need to sleep." He turned to Barry the Beaver. "Show my valiant friend to one of the beds where he can sleep."

Benjamin reluctantly followed the beaver. He didn't think he needed to sleep and he didn't want to miss a moment in this delightful place. In spite of these thoughts, however, shortly after he had lain down in the thoroughly comfortable bed, Benjamin was fast asleep. He slept for several hours. He had hopped a long way and met many challenges since he had first arrived.

He awoke to find Obedience sitting beside him, once again waiting to lead him to the king.

"Ah Benjamin," said the king, when he saw Benjamin. "Come before me." Benjamin hopped to where the king sat. Decisive was sitting beside the throne, on his cushion, and Glowing One was close by. They both nodded and smiled at Benjamin. The room fell silent.

"I am giving you a new name," the Great King told Benjamin. "When you are in this kingdom, you will be known as Valiant Friend, because that is what you have been to me."

Benjamin bowed and said "Thank you, Your Majesty. I will always be your Valiant Friend whenever you have need of me."

"Yes, I know that, Valiant Friend. You were told by Obedience that you would have the dearest wish of your heart after you had completed the task I would ask of you. You performed well, my Valiant Friend. What would you like as your reward?'

"Your Majesty, there is something. I would like a froggy friend, as I am the only frog in my pond. However I would also like to stay in this kingdom and serve you."

The king answered very kindly. "My Valiant Friend, you will indeed live in my kingdom, but not yet. For now you must return to your pond. You can serve me there by continuing to be kind and helpful to the other animals and by telling them about me and about your quest. Some will not believe you, but tell them anyway. They need to hear. One day, I will call you and then you will come and live with me in this kingdom."

"Your Majesty, there is one question I would like to ask before I return to my pond."

"What is your question?" asked the king.

"Why was Wickedness not ugly, like his servants?"

"Wickedness looks appealing and attractive on the outside. You do not see him as he really is. That is why so many are tricked into following him."

Benjamin then sadly took leave of the Great King.

CHAPTER 14

Obedience led him back through the huge entrance past the climbing water, back to the forest.

As he came closer to his pond once again looking forward to sitting on his favourite lily pad and to seeing all his friends, he heard a strange noise. He had never before heard that noise, and he wondered what it could possibly be. As he came closer it grew louder until he came within sight of the pond, and realized that there were many frogs hopping around, waiting for him to arrive. The noise he had heard had been these frogs singing and croaking to each other.

"I asked for a froggy friend," he said to Obedience in amazement. "He's given me a whole pondful!"

Obedience laughed. "The king always gives us more than we ever expect. He loves to surprise us. Good-bye, Valiant Friend Benjamin. I must return now to the kingdom of the Great King."

"Goodbye, Obedience, my good friend. I hope we shall meet again, some day."

"Oh, I'm sure we will," answered Obedience. With that, she turned, waved to Benjamin and made her way back through the forest.

Benjamin hopped happily to join his new friends on his pond. On his favourite lily pad, he saw a very pretty lady frog, waiting for him to join her.

From that day, Benjamin, now Valiant Friend, never felt lonely again, and told all his friends at the pond about the Great King. Some didn't believe him, but many did, and loved to hear him tell the story again and again, which he loved to do.

One afternoon, as he sat on his favourite pad with his pretty lady frog, whose name was Lily, Benjamin saw Obedience standing by the edge of the pond.

Valiant Friend, the Great King has need of you, once again," she said.

"May I come too?" asked Lily.

"Yes, you may," answered Obedience

"But when I am gone, who will tell the story of Valiant Friend and the Great King?" asked Benjamin.

"The Great King has already taken care of that,' answered Obedience, and as he and Lily hopped away with Obedience, he heard the mummy and daddy frogs and other mummy and daddy animals telling their children the story of Valiant Friend and the Great King.

Code key

The code key is:

D E F G H I J K L M N O P Q R S T U V W X Y Z
A B C

A B C D E F G H I J K L M N O P Q R S T U V W
X Y Z

Printed in the United States
By Bookmasters